THE GUILD

By: Anny Omous

Publishing & Credit Notes

Published by Anny Omous Publishing

Anny Omous Publishing, 1305 Skyline Drive, Katrine, Ontario, Canada, P0A 1L0

Distributed by Lulu.com

Published in this first edition 2015

Copyright © Anny Omous Publishing, 2015

Library and Archives Canada Cataloguing in Publication

Omous-Anny/2015

The Guild/Anny Omous

ISBN 978-0-9938933-2-2

EBook ISBN 978-0-9938933-3-9

Cover design and photography: Brian Boudreau Photography

Tattoo by: Caleb Atkinson, Dead City Studios

Formatting by: Natasha MacDonald

Copy Edited by: William LaRochelle

www.threeyearaffair.wordpress.com

Dedication

To the Angel that feeds my demons,

Know this, they are always ravenous, and never sated.

INTRO

I could smell the meat as it simmered in the sauce on the stove; as I heard the door open and close behind me. I didn't turn to greet him. I heard his footsteps as he casually walked up behind me. His lips softly caressed the back of my neck, as I stirred the dinner I was preparing. I felt his hands on my shoulders as they slowly slid down my arms and made their way onto my midriff; one turning upwards and one turning south, as he pulled me into his embrace. I let out a deep breath as I turned my head, allowing his lips to move down the right side of my neck. I could feel his hands grabbing at the bottom of my skirt, pulling it upwards and stroking the inside of my thigh.

"How was your day?" he whispered in my ear.

"Long." I respond back leaning my body into his and turning my head to meet his gaze. "How was yours?"

"Taxing," he said in a long breathy drawl. "What are you making?"

I turned my body towards him. His hand at the bottom of my back holding me as I leaned away from him, teasing. "Thai," I answer looking him in the eyes. I dipped my finger into the sauce and ever so gently removed it from my finger with my mouth. "It's kinda sweet. Wanna taste?"

"Yep!" He responded smiling ever so sweetly, his eyes never leaving mine.

Once again I soak my finger in the sauce. I bring it to his full lips and allow him to sample a taste. He looks at me, pleased. His eyes piercing through me.

I felt my back hit the island behind me as he leaned over me and kissed me hard. I saw his long arm reach out and turn the burner off on the stove.

"Aren't you hungry?" I ask.

"Yeah, I'm hungry." He replied, "I'm hungry for you."

Chapter One

Peter stood at the customs gate with anticipation. The year and a half apart from Anny had made him realize how much he missed her. He stood nervously holding a dozen roses, awaiting the sight of her face. Feeling self- conscious in front of the three other members of the club he had brought with him, he tried to redeem himself and said, "Bitches are always fucking late right?"

The large prospect to his right half-grinned and nodded in agreement. It had been club policy the last few months that any upholding titled member of the table have a security detail with them in any public venue. The war between the

God's Hammer club and theirs had reached an all-time high and the body count was rising.

Peter scanned the crowd hard as people started to filter out of the gate. He came across a familiar face and smiled. He walked towards Cassy as she embraced her husband Chris.

"Hey Cassy. Good to see you. What happened? Did Anny get searched?" Peter giggled jokingly.

Cassy whirled at Peter with a grim look. She paused for a second as she released Chris from her arms and walked toward Peter, motioning him to a more private area, "I'm so sorry Peter. She didn't come with me. She's not here. I'm sorry." Cassy responded, trying her hardest to present the news as gently as she could.

"What do you mean she didn't come with you? She didn't come back to Canada? Is she okay? What the hell is going on, Cassy?" Peter said.

"No… she came back to Canada. She just didn't come back to Toronto with me. She left. I don't know where she is. I'm sorry." Cassy said and then turned to walk away.

Peter grabbed her by her arm as she turned from him and pulled her into him close. "What the fuck do you mean she just left? Bullshit! You know where she is. Where the fuck is she?" He snarled under his breath at her.

"Let go of my arm, Peter. You're hurting me. I really don't know where she is. But I think there's someone else. I'm sorry to be the one to tell you that. I think you guys are over. That's all I know. Now let me go," Cassy said, bargaining with him.

"Is everything all right, babe?" said Chris, who had come over, noticing the small altercation that was under way with Peter and his wife.

"No, everything is not okay, buddy." Peter boomed at Chris. "Your fucking wife here knows something and won't tell me, but she's gonna. You fucking bitches cluck like hens with gossip. Just tell me where she is and we can all just go home." He shouted at Cassy.

"Look man, I don't know what's happening here but obviously if my wife says she doesn't know then she doesn't. Now take your hand off of her or we are going to have a problem," Chris authoritatively asserted. He grabbed Cassy's other arm in an attempt to pull her and walk away from the situation. As he turned, he realized that a small half circle of Peter's entourage had blocked his exit. He turned and faced Peter who had yet to release Cassy from his grip. Peter smiled and then started to laugh quietly. "Sure buddy, just a misunderstanding. No worries." He said calmly and let go of Cassy.

"Yeah okay, no problem. It's been a long day for everyone." Chris said and extended his hand towards Peter to shake it. Peter accepted his hand and as he shook it pulled him in and whispered, "Threaten me again and I'll fucking kill you asshole."

Chris looked up at him, and as he did Peter with all his strength head-butted him. A flood of pain and blood overwhelmed Chris and his face. He dropped to the ground and felt his ribs take another impact, this time from Peter's steel toed riding boot. He heard Cassy scream and the sound of the group's footsteps increase in pace upon departure from the scene as he tried to regain his breath.

Peter reefed on Cassy's arm, pulling it behind her back and upwards. Maintaining, his control on her he rushed her through the airport. "Boss, what the fuck are we doing?" said the younger prospect to Peter.

"This bitch is coming with us. Just follow my lead. You all go ahead of us and get the van from the Valet, and be ready." Peter instructed them. The men did as they were told and rushed off to secure the vehicle.

"Peter I'm sorry. Please let me go. I don't know anything."
Cassy pleaded with him, the sound of fear vibrating
through her voice. Her arm throbbed from the force Peter
held on her.

"Don't worry, sweet heart. We're just gonna take a little
ride to somewhere we can talk. I'm gonna ask you a few
questions and when you tell me what I want to know then
you can go home." Peter said to her in a low tone, still
pressing her to move fast through the crowded airport.

"I'm not going with you. Let me go!" Cassy yelled and tried
to free herself from his grip. People had started to look at
them as she struggled to free herself. Peter with one quick
movement spun her around and slapped her hard across
the face, bringing her to her knees. The crowd hushed and
was taken aback. Peter quickly gathered himself and knelt
down, flopped Cassy over his shoulder in a fireman's hold
and ran out the front doors before anyone in the crowd
could gather themselves to react to the situation.

Outside the doors, he scanned the cars impatiently, aware
of the impending altercation that would occur between
security and himself if his team left him hanging. The black
van squealed to a stop in front of him. The back door was
flung open and he threw Cassy into the van as quick as he

could before attempting to enter the van himself. He felt a hand on his shoulder and heard a low voice behind him asking him to turn around. Peter turned quickly and sized up the large airport security officer before hitting him with all his might in the stomach. The officer dropped, and Peter dove into the van yelling, "Drive! Drive! Drive!"

The tires smoked as they took off, leaving the scrambling security officers in a cloud. "Where to now boss?" The driver asked.

Peter caught his breath while he thought for a second, then said, "The cabin."

Chapter Two

*T*he cabin was one of the many safe houses owned by the club. Nestled in the Almaguin Highlands a mere two and a half hour drive from the city, it was a perfect refuge from any watchful eyes. It sat on a two hundred acre parcel of land and had only seasonal road access. The title to the land was listed to a strip club owner in the city with whom the Devil's Cradle had become silent partners. The cabin was only used for club business and by titled members only. The land had a few outbuildings, a pond and plenty of hardwood acres of bush. The nearest neighbour was a ten-minute walk, and in an area made up of people in retirement or looking for privacy and escape from the city, it was a perfect place to have privacy to conduct any business that needed the shield of silence.

The cabin itself was small in nature housing a single bedroom, and a one room living room-slash-kitchen area with a large stone fireplace. Designed in a simpler time, it had no electricity or running water, but did have a root cellar that was accessible by a panel in the floor in the kitchen. The cellar had no windows and a dirt floor. It smelt of must and mould. The cellar had been transformed into a perfect holding cell for anyone the club thought needed a little encouragement and time to expel any information it deemed necessary that someone may be withholding under the guise of morality.

Cassy sat in the dankness of the cellar unaware if it had been two days or three that she had been held captive. Her body ached from the punishment she had received from Peter when she was unable to answer his line of questioning regarding Anny and her whereabouts. Though she cursed Anny for her predicament she couldn't help to wonder why this friend she held so close had lived a life she never knew, and all at once she understood why Anny had fled. Her mind turned to her husband. God how she missed him. Certainly the police were looking for her by now. *Anytime they would be there to save her. Wouldn't they?* She kept that thought in her mind, picturing them there to take her home, the only place she wanted to be.

Her legs were numb from the coldness of the ground and though she feared what may be rustling in the darkness around her she feared it less than the next time she would be called for questioning, which most certainly would be soon. She tried to hold her tears of fear back and remain as silent as possible as she heard the footsteps above her and scraping of chairs being moved. She strained to make out what the muffled voices above her were saying, praying that they would forget her existence below them.

As she heard the creaking of the hatch opening, chills ran up her spine. She turned her head and leaned her body into the dampness of the rock wall foundation willing herself to disappear into it and become invisible. "Hello darling. It's time to talk again," she heard Peter say in a low tone. "Come on, up and at em."

She pulled herself up and tried to maintain her composure as Peter extended his hand towards her. He helped her as she weakly climbed the stairs into the light, so bright it blinded her. He escorted her to the table and chair that she had become accustomed to as her throne of despair.

Peter circled her slowly. Staring at her like prey. Inside he had started to question if she was telling the truth about not knowing Anny's whereabouts, but he had come to a point of no turning back. He knew he had maybe one or more interrogations with her until she succumbed to her injuries or he would have to end this with or without answers. This was not a reality he wanted to accept.

"Cassy, I know that this last while we have spent together has not been comfortable for you. I know you miss your family and want to see them. I want that too. I'm not a man without family values. That's why this is happening. Anny needs to come home to her family. She needs to atone for her actions and explain why she would choose anything else but her family. I think even if you do not know where she is you can come up with a solution as to how we may figure that out. Do you have any ideas as to how sweetheart?" He said in a sweet tone.

"I don't know. I'm so tired. I don't know." Cassy whimpered. Peter grabbed her by the back of the neck and forced her head onto the table hard. He pulled a hunting knife from its sheath from his belt and garnered it to her face. Spit landed on her face as he shouted into her ear, "Well fucking think!"

He released her from his grip and grabbed her hand, placing it on the table, holding it at her wrist. Tears started to run down her face as her mind raced trying to come up with a solution. She looked up at the three other men in the room and noticed one of them casually playing on his cell phone. Peter slowly pressed the knife hard into her pinky finger drawing the knife across it in a saw like motion, drawing blood. Cassy screamed out, "Wait I know! I know how to find her!"

Peter pulled the knife away and let her hand go. "How?" he asked her. "Facebook .... I can message her and ask. It may even show where she is."

She answered suddenly animated with a glimmer of hope of surviving the situation. "Do you have Facebook and messenger on your phone?" She posed the question to the young prospect who she had observed playing on his cell.

"Yeah!" he responded.

"Well fucking give her you phone!" Peter yelled at him.

Bashfully, he handed Cassy his cell. Peter stood behind her as she logged herself in to Facebook. She checked to see if Anny was available for chat and let out a sigh, "She's on here. Let me message her and see if she will respond."

"Do it," Peter said, trying to appear calm.

Hey girl. What's up? Where are you?

Cassy messaged Anny.

Time seemed to stop as Cassy awaited a reply from Anny.
She could hear her heart pounding and wondered if the
others in the room could as well.

Finally she heard the popping sound of Anny typing a
response.

**Doing well. Can't talk right now but will call you soon.
Sorry I had to bail like that. Hope you and Chris are
having fun. Miss you! Luv ya! I will explain everything
when I call.**

Anny responded.

"How the fuck does that help?" Peter screamed at Cassy.

"Look right here," Cassy pointed at the phone, "it says sent
from Winnipeg Manitoba, right here."

Peter grabbed the phone from Cassy's hand and stared at it.
All at once, he pieced it together, "Sneaky Fucking Bitch!!"
Peter's mind flashed back to a moment not too long
before. A moment that had stuck with him and always
bothered him. He rubbed his left hand as he recalled his
time spent under interrogation with the large beast of a cop

named Inspector Woods. The man he remembered that seemed to know Anny and her business better than just through surveillance. It had always bothered him that he had addressed her as Anny and not Annabella like any other cop that had mentioned her. It also had made him wonder how he had known about his and Annys' altercation on Christmas Eve when she had found him with the whore he was enjoying. Most of all it had always bothered him that the Inspector had seemed so enraged when he had told him that Anny was being a fucking bitch and deserved what she got, that he had felt it necessary to dislocate Peters' thumb and break his two of his fingers. It had taken two other officers to remove the man off of him. Peter was certain that it would have escalated if they had not arrived when they had. Now he knew. It all made sense. His rage was spewing out of him. The humiliation of her actions would not go unpunished. Their years together and everything they had been through only to be betrayed.

He whipped the phone against the wall, smashing it into pieces. "FUCKING WHORE! FUCK! FUCK! FUCK!!" He screamed smashing his fists off the table. "I'm gonna fucking kill her!" he shrilled before driving the hunting knife into the table, just missing Cassy's hand.

He turned his back to the others and faced the wall. His shoulders moved up and down like an animal trying to breathe out its rage. Cassy sank down into her chair avoiding eye contact with any of the men in the room, trying not to make a sound.

"Boss, what do we now? Do we let her go?" asked the large prospect.

Peter let out a long sigh and paused for the longest time. Still facing the wall, he responded, "Call Sonny. Get him here now. If he gives you any hell just tell him it's about Anny."

"Okay, I'm on it." He said and then exited the cabin to make the call.

"What about her, and my phone?" the young prospect asked. "Do I bring her home?"

"Fuck your phone dip shit!" Peter snarled and then turned around. "No I got a better idea."

He reefed the knife from the table, grabbed Cassy's hand and pinned it down. "You're gonna ensure she comes home, beautiful," he said as he pierced the knife into Cassy's pinky. Cassy looked at him in horror and screamed, "Oh my god! No! No! Please no!"

Chapter Three

*L*iam's phone had rung for the third time when he finally pulled himself away to answer it. I could hear him talking in the other room in a serious tone.

"Damn it!" He said upon entering the room, "I gotta go. Some fucking emergency at work. Sorry, we'll have to pick up where we left off when I get back."

He grabbed me close, his hands on the bottom of my back pulling me into him, and leaned down to kiss me. I pulled away teasing and said "Fine, but don't be too long or I may forget where we left off."

"I doubt that very much." He said, giggling and then kissed me softly before grabbing his things and heading out the door.

I laid back on the bed, enjoying the quiet, thinking of our last two weeks together. It had been blissful, perfect and I had no regrets on the choice I had made to be with him. His kind demeanour and sweetness was a change of pace from my old life, one I surely did not miss. I hadn't spoken with Peter and certainly by now he had figured it out that I had no intention on doing so. I stared out the window for the longest time, enjoying the peaceful feeling in my heart before deciding on a shower.

I stood in the shower, allowing the heat of the water to penetrate the skin on my back, remembering where we had left off in the other room. I could still feel his breath on the back of my neck and his hands slowly moving up my body as he pulled me into him. I used my soapy fingers to retrace his steps taking my own breath away in the process. Suddenly I was pulled out of my moment by the sound of the front door opening and closing. *Liam must have forgot something* I thought to myself, as I quickly finished rinsing off. I shut off the shower, wrapped myself in the black silk robe I had purchased in Japan, and headed to the kitchen to see him.

"Couldn't wait?" I said as I entered the kitchen, and then stopped dead in my tracks. Panic rushed through my body and I froze for a second before recovering my breath enough to spout out, "FUCK!"

My Uncle Sonny stood there smiling with a look a serial killer gives before the torture begins. I turned to run but he caught the back of my hair. "Where the fuck do you think you're going, sweetheart." He said, laughing, pulling my hair so hard my chin was forced toward the ceiling. "I almost didn't recognize you, but you are looking a lot more like your bitch whore mother these days."

I could feel my feet clumsily being pushed forward hard and the impact of my face hitting the wall made me see spots. The blood had started to run from my cheek as he pushed himself into me and whispered in my ear, "I was so happy Peter chose me for this trip. I still owe you from the bar. You remember that, you little cunt? Well I can promise you this is gonna hurt a fuck of a lot more than that.

"Where's the old man?" he screamed at me.

"He's not here! He's not here!" I yelled back.

"Bullshit, don't you fucking lie to me. Here piggy, pig, pig."

He shouted out, as he swung me around, leading me to the hallway.

"He's not fucking here, asshole!" I screeched back. "He got called into work. You're fucking lucky he did, or you'd be dead by now."

He thrusted me back into the kitchen and through to the living room, bouncing me off the walls in the process. I could feel the pain shooting through my body with every impact and the drywall cracking on the last wall. Finally he released me from his grip with a shove to the ground that sent my body bouncing across the floor. A hard crack of my body being stopped by the large wood coffee table left me gasping for air. I let out a cry as I tried to pull myself up, coughing and trying to fill my lungs back with air. It was too late, he had made it to me before I could get my bearings. He grabbed me by the throat and looked me dead in the eyes by only inches away and screamed, "You think I'm afraid of some fucking cop, you cunt? I'm gonna fucking kill him. He should be so lucky. I wouldn't wish upon anyone what's in store for you. You fucking piece-of-shit rat." I heard a crack from the impact of my head hitting the coffee table and then blackness.

Chapter Four

What's going on?" said Liam to the Constable clipping at his heals as he made his way through the office.

"We got some intel, boss," said the short man trying to keep up with Liam's long strides." It's from Ontario. There was a delay that might have screwed us out of keeping on the trail. It's about Peter Wilson and the Devil's Cradle club."

Liam stopped in his tracks, the Constable behind him bumping into him in the process. "Why am I just hearing about this now? You know I am to be notified right away when we have intel on that piece of shit! Follow me to the board room. Grab anyone that has a hand in this. I want all the details... NOW!"

As the Constable scurried to round-up the necessary people for the meeting, Liam could feel his blood pressure rising. He made his way to the boardroom and seated himself at the end of the long table. His blood was boiling and the anticipation of the information was nearly too much for him to contain.

"Sir, I apologize for the delay, but we have just received the information from Ontario. It seems that there was a long delay due to the process of which identifying Mr. Wilson took place. It has passed through a number of different channels before reaching our unit." said the shaky Constable that had been following his footsteps.

"Constable Black, get on with it," snarled Liam at the incompetence he had assumed had occurred.

"Well Sir, we have received news that Peter Wilson has been positively identified as a perpetrator in an abduction and assault at Toronto Pearson Airport two weeks ago. He is wanted for questioning and they have enough to press charges at this time. We have video surveillance from the airport that a witness and the victim of the assault identified him from. Unfortunately the time it took for it to travel through the hands of the Pearson Airport Security to the Toronto Metro Police to the Ontario Provincial Police to our task force was the issue. The situation at hand is as such. An individual named Cassy Abraham landed at Pearson on June 28th. She was greeted by her husband Chris Abraham. She was then confronted by Peter Wilson. Apparently Cassy Abraham had just arrived from being abroad with Peter Wilson's girlfriend Anny Omous. Anny Omous did not arrive with Cassy Abraham. A confrontation then took place. Peter Wilson then did assault Mr. Chris Abraham and is seen in the video surveillance leaving with Mrs. Cassy Abraham. The surveillance video shows that a struggle between Mrs. Abraham and Mr. Wilson did occur and it looks to be that she left the airport not on her own accord. At this time the whereabouts of both Mrs. Cassy Abraham and Mr. Peter Wilson are unknown. Our joint task force in Toronto currently has surveillance on all of the known clubs' residences but has not secured any information that would constitute a search warrant at this time. We have secured information that Ms. Anny Omous did arrive in Canada on June 28th to Vancouver International Airport. However she changed her destination at the last minute to the city of Winnipeg. We have no further information with regards to her whereabouts, but we have started questioning the cab companies and hotels in the city with hopes of finding her whereabouts or at least start to establish a time line since her arrival here. I will now start the surveillance tape where we can see Mr. Wilson and some of his known associates commit the said crimes in question."

The Constable then turned off the lights to the room and motioned for his co-worker to start the video surveillance. Liam sat frozen, glued to his chair. A sinking feeling rooted him in his there. *Oh my god! What have we done?...* was all he could think. He tried to concentrate on the screen ahead as he watched the violence unfold in front of his eyes. His inner thoughts were on fire. *What am I gonna do? What do I do with Anny? How are we gonna make it out of this? It's just a matter of time until someone figures out she's with me. I am fucked!*

As the video came to an end Liam composed himself. "Thank you, Constable Black. I want two teams out canvassing. Never mind the unis I want my team out there; one questioning the cab companies, one at the hotels. I want a team to organize any information on Cassy Abraham with regards to electronic information. Has she been on any social networking, or made any phone calls? I want to know if she pissed in the bathroom before departing the plane. Constable Black, I want you to go over the interviews that occurred between the different channels and Chris Abraham. If there is anything, and I mean anything you believe left unquestioned that may be deemed pertinent to this investigation, I want you to call him and find out. Any information comes in to me first. I will decide what is necessary to follow up on or not. Is this understood? Now before I rip a new asshole into the department head of the Ontario unit responsible for the delay, is there any other new information regarding the Devils Cradle club that I am unaware of since my time away from the office?" he asked.

"Um... Um." the Constable stuttered shaking looking through his papers.

"SPIT IT OUT, CONSTABLE BLACK!" Liam yelled.

"Just ... just, um, sorry sir, we received information that Sonny Omous is in town. He was spotted yesterday downtown. The plates were run from the bike he was riding and it was identified as his by the local 549 detachment. Unfortunately we received the information too late to get a tail on him, and his whereabouts at this time are unknown." the Constable managed to get out in response.

"Jesus Fucking Christ," Liam let slip out with horror in his tone. He got up, grabbed his jacket and bolted from the room. Running through the office the only thought screaming through his head was, *Oh my god, Anny!*

Chapter Five

My Uncle Sonny was a sociopath. I hadn't seen him in years and had not wanted to. The mix of his personality and his gladiator type build made him as dangerous as they came. He was a second-run enforcer for the club. If you hadn't given them what they had wanted after the first round they came knocking, Sonny would be sent for a visit. To this day I have never heard of a third visit being necessary. His cruelty superseded him and he was nick-named Son of Satan, although no one ever called him that to his face. He lacked any ability to empathize with anyone and the only time I ever saw him smile or look excited was during times

of extreme violence upon the poor bastard that he decided
had looked at him wrong. He had an unusual game that he
played with his wife, based solely on humiliation and
random beatings.

Although he was the unfaithful one, he crudely named his
only son Chance. He would laugh and tell people that it
was because his wife was such a whore there was a good
chance that it wasn't his son. This of course started after a
partial facial reconstruction surgery that she had required
after an evening of hell with him. I do think it was his way
to validate the extreme attack upon her. The evening at the
bar that Sonny had brought up was in fact the last time I
had been alone in his presence without protection.

My cousin Chance had come to the clubhouse to see his
father, which at the time did not seem unusual. He was
always coming in to beg his father for money for food for
him and his mother. This time, however, he had come in a
fit of rage. He had seen enough of his mother's beatings,
and after discovering how a conversation about the brand
of coffee she had bought went down earlier that day, he
wanted vengeance. At the time he was only twenty-one and
full of piss and vinegar. I was seated with some of the other
old ladies waiting for Peter to arrive and drinking beers.
Chance had made the error of underestimating his father's
natural instinct for anticipating an ambush. The boy had

started to run towards him, picking up a bottle and smashing it along the way. Sonny grabbed him, picked him up in the air, and slammed him down so hard on the table that it broke and they both crashed to the ground. Sonny had retrieved the smashed bottle from Chance's hands and was garnering as a weapon to his throat. I knew he was gonna kill him. I jumped on his back and was punching him in the head. It gave Chance just enough time to wriggle free of his grip. Unfortunately, it turned Sonny's attention towards me. I didn't realize at first that he had stabbed me in the stomach with the bottle. To be honest, it felt more like a really   hard punch. He was on top of me, hitting me over and over again in the face. Chance picked up a chair and broke it over his head, rendering him unconscious. He helped me up and we bailed. We got his mother and him out of town before Sonny made it home and they never came back.

 Chance and I had stayed in touch secretly over the years. His way of rebellion was to open a tattoo shop of which his clientele were primarily the members of the Hammer of God club, our rivals. He even befriended the president of their central Ontario chapter's son Justin. We had spent some time together shortly before I had gone abroad and he had been the one to give me my beautiful tattoo. Luckily my stab wound was superficial, leaving only a few scars, and it didn't take long to heal. The only reason Sonny had not retaliated was due to the protection that my Uncle Tom had ensured for me and as well Peter, (although Peter idealized him and his tactics).

"Wake up, sweetheart. Wake up. No time for sleeping now. We've just gotten started" I heard Sonny said in a strangely sweet manner as I slowly stirred to consciousness.

My eyes were just adjusting to the light and I could barely see out of them from the swelling, as I lifted my head. A pang of pain shot through my head and face from the spot my head had been smashed off the table. I had tunnel vision and couldn't talk, though I could taste the blood in my mouth. I tried to spit it out but my swollen lips could not project it far enough away from my mouth, so it slowly ran down my face. I felt a hard sting as his hand met my face with a hard slap. "I said wake the fuck up!"

My head flew to the side and landed on the ground again.

"Get up or I will fucking make sure you can't bitch." I heard him snap at me. I struggled to get my arms underneath me. Shaking, I was roughly propped upright by them, "How did you find me?" I asked half-whispering.

"Oh yeah," He laughed "I forgot. I have a gift for you complements of your old man...sorry ex old man, right, you whore." He reached into his pocket and pulled out a jewellery box and threw it at me, at the same time balancing a 357 magnum handgun on his knee. I swayed myself up to a kneeling position and tried a few attempts to pick it up. My hands were shaking as I tried to undo the red ribbon wrapped around the box. Finally, I had it available to open. I opened the box and stared inside. It took me only a few seconds to realize the gravity of it's contents. Inside sat a pinky finger. A pinky finger so delicately placed on top of the grey silk lining of the box. A pinky finger that had just been manicured and painted a pale pink. The pale pink that I had watched Cassy so carefully pick out from the many other hues of pink at the spa. I dropped the box on to the floor in horror.

"Where is she? What have you done? You fucking animals!" I screamed at him. My face was met with another impact. This time his boot hit my already swollen cheek. The pain shot through my entire body. I laid shaking and crying on the floor in front of him.

"You always needed to be taught respect. Your father was too sweet on you. I told him that," he sneered at me.

I heard the ring of a cell phone. He put the gun down on the end table beside him and answered it. I could hear him answering a line of questions in one word responses when my eyes focused in on the bottom shelf of the coffee table. There lay my only chance of hope for survival. A letter opener, the small blade-shaped object shone in the sunlight that was beaming through the living room window. I could hear in his voice the conversation was coming to a close. Ever so cautiously, I rolled myself over slowly to slide the letter opener into my hand and tucked it in toward my body. I brought my hands inwards to my stomach and slowly rolled over in an attempt to make it back up to a kneeling position again, concealing the object in my hands.

"Yeah. K. No worries, she's not fucking going anywhere. Yeah," I hear him say and then end the call. "Well, lucky for you I think Peter still has a soft spot for you. Either that or he wants to make sure he gets his round in. In either case, he has given me the full green light to have some fun, as long as you can still talk apparently, and still have your tits we are okay. Maybe he wants to cut them off himself." He said, smiling at me with dead eyes for a moment before carrying on.

"So where were we? Oh ya teaching you some respect. You know that was something I always used to give your father hell for. The amount of disrespect he took from your whore mother. She was always flaunting herself around the club. Then, to start fucking that pig cop." He said softly, pausing to light a smoke, and then continued." I told him that you probably weren't his. If you hadn't have looked so much like him he might have listened. Fucking whore. It was me you know, who he came to that night. I told him what he had to do, what he needed to do in order to keep the club from falling apart. He didn't want to but I told him if he didn't the rest of the club would view him as weak and leave just like Jack had. I told him that we would all leave and go patch over with Jack. He did what he needed to do. He shouldn't have left you alive. You turned out just like her; disloyal, disrespectful and a slut."

With that, he spat in my face. "I am going to show you what disrespect gets you sweet heart." He said and then rose to a standing position.

 I sat kneeling in front of him swaying, trying to find my centre of balance as my head was pounding. I knew this was my moment and I had only one shot. He grabbed the hair at the top of my head and wound up his fist to bring down upon me. In that half a second, I struck. Lifting myself just enough to get propulsion, I took the blade-shaped object and thrust it with all my might into his crotch. I heard him groan and saw the blood starting to pool in his pants before receiving the full force of his blow.

My body hit the floor with ultimate force. I looked up to see him grabbing his groin in pain. I lunged at the end table, grabbing the gun. When he realized what I was doing, he let go of his bloody appendage and snagged me. As we were falling backwards toward the floor, I could feel his hands grabbing, trying to remove the gun from my grip when my finger found the trigger. What must have been less than a few seconds felt like forever. I heard the bang of the initial shot. The shot so loud it left my ears ringing. I couldn't stop; another five bangs. He laid dead weight on top of me. My finger still pulling the trigger though no bullets were left to fire. I half rolled him off of me. He was gasping for air but instead only a mist of red was escaping his mouth onto my face. I could feel the warmth of his blood penetrating through my robe and onto my chest.

"Fucking cunt," He managed to whisper before his breath ceased. Half-pinned under him, I felt my rage boil up. I reached for the letter opener and then plunged it repeatedly into him, crying and screaming over and over again "Fuck you! Fuck you! Fuck You!"

Suddenly I was being pulled out from under him. I was delirious and thrashing at the person pulling me away from him. "No! Baby no! No! No! No! No baby! I'm so sorry baby!" I hear Liam say as he cradled me and rocked me in his arms. "I'm so sorry baby! I'm so sorry!"

Chapter Six

J ust breathe, baby. Just breathe," Liam said softly, cradling
Anny in his arms. His hand held her arms on her stomach,
as he rocked her back and forth. Tears ran down his cheeks
as he used his free hand, attempting to wipe the blood
from her almost unrecognizable face. He kissed her softly
on the forehead. Feeling the tension subside from her
body he said again, "Just breathe."

Movement from outside the large picture window grabbed
his attention. Some of the neighbours had started to come
out of their houses, curious of the noise from the struggle.
He managed to compose himself enough to realize the

gravity of their situation and the events that would soon fall upon them. He lifted Anny from the ground and placed her in the sitting position on the chair.

"Anny, we gotta go. We gotta go now," he said panicking as he tried to keep his voice calm between staggered breaths. He looked around the room trying to figure out his next steps. He picked up the 357 revolver and wiped it off with his shirt, placing his hand in the gun leaving his finger prints and did the same with the letter opener that Anny had so crudely been using as a weapon. He grabbed a blanket from the back of the couch and wrapped it around her shoulders, kneeling in front of her, he said, "Baby, we gotta go. Stay with me. We gotta leave now."

As he started to lift her from the chair to a standing position he heard the ring of a cell phone. Scanning the floor in front of him he couldn't seem to find the source. He reached under the couch, and pulled out the phone. Unsteadily, he answered it. "Sonny, the boys will be there in a half an hour. Wait there for that fucking pig and take care of him." He heard a voice from the other end say. He stayed silent on his end of the line. "Sonny?" He heard the voice question. "Sonny, you there?"

There was a pause and a then a loud breath that vibrated over the line. "Anny, where's Sonny?"

"He's dead!" Liam responded and then hung up the phone. He shoved the phone into his pocket and grabbed Anny under his arm, dragging her out the door to the Suburban parked in the driveway. He placed her in the passenger seat and buckled her in. "Anny, stay with me baby." he said.

He could hear the sirens in the distance and the voices in the crowd buzzing as he disconnected the GPS and the LOJACK on the vehicle and then started it. The tires squealed as he reversed out of the driveway, swinging the vehicle and then stomping on the gas to reach maximum acceleration.

"Anny stay awake!" He said as he gently tapped her face, swerving the vehicle in the process. "Come on! Stay awake! "He heard her quietly moan. "Come on look at me." He saw her try and open her blackened eyes. "That's good baby! Look at me! Stay with me!" he said gently.

Swerving in and out of traffic on the freeway, heading out of the city he realized he needed to slow down. He adjusted his speed and blended into traffic. *Fuck! Fuck! Fuck!* His inner voice was screaming at him. His heart was racing and his mind was speeding through the list of actions that could be his next move. *Fuck!*

"Where are we going?" he heard Anny try and say through her swollen lips. "Somewhere safe. Just stay with me. Don't fall asleep. Stay with me," he said in response.

He heard his cell phone vibrate and looked down on the console to see the name Sargent Dalahan flashing on his screen. *Fuck, they already know,* was all he could think. He looked up and saw a freeway sign that showed a blue hospital notification. Throwing the wheel of the vehicle hard to the right, cutting off the traffic behind him, he reached the off-ramp. Entering the hospital parking lot he found a parking spot and put the vehicle into park. Clumsily handling the phone, he dialled the missed call back.

"Inspector Woods where the hell are you?" he heard Sergeant Dalahan yell into the phone.

"Sir I am at East General Hospital," he responded.

"What the fuck are you doing there? What is going on? I got two detachments at your house now and a chopper in the air. The journalists are already at your house. What am I supposed to tell them?" He yelled into the phone.

"Sir, I have Anny Omous with me. I have kept this quiet, but she has been a C.I. for me. She came to me and I was keeping her protected to ensure the investigation would not be compromised. I believe we have a mole in our department. I should have told you but I was unsure of anyone and anything. I reached my home after being notified today that Sonny Omous was in town to find him assaulting her. An altercation between himself and I occurred that lead to his death. Anny Omous is in need of urgent medical attention. I will be leaving her here at the hospital to be looked after and then heading north of the city. I have made contact with Peter Wilson via Sonny Omous' cell phone. It is a burner phone, sir. Untraceable. He has asked for a meet in order to discuss the release of Cassy Abraham. I must leave immediately in order to attend this meet and will contact you with my position as soon as I have secured the location," Liam responded to his superior in an aggressive manner.

"No Inspector Woods! YOU WILL STAND DOWN! Stay with Miss. Omous. We need to ensure that this does not end up as a media shit show! I cannot believe that you did not reveal this information to me. STAND DOWN! Do you hear me?" Sargent Dalahan yelled. "No, Sir! I cannot and I will not!" Liam responded and then hung up the phone. He stepped out of the vehicle and threw the phone onto a grass hill on the edge of the parking lot. Returning to the vehicle, he ran his hand across Anny's face gently and said, "Don't worry, baby. I just sent them on a goose chase."

He put the vehicle in drive and sped out of the parking lot, heading east, knowing he was on borrowed time.

Chapter Seven

As Liam crossed the Ontario border, he could no longer ignore Anny's cries. She had been writhing in pain for the last hour, slipping in and out of consciousness. He looked hopelessly for a sign showing a store for supplies and a way off the highway. Surely by now an APB had been issued for his vehicle. His only strong hold of the disabled GPS and LOJACK was not going to last forever. He needed a new plan. "It's okay Anny! Look at me."

He looked down to see tears running from her eyes as she rocked back in forth in pain. Knowing he needed to focus her, he said to her in a sweet tone, "Tell me the story of your favourite moment between us."

"I already told you this story a few times," Anny replied softly, half awake.

"I forget." He said, "Tell me again."

"Okay." She managed to say between groans. She closed her eyes and proceeded to tell him. "After the reunion, we met for dinner when you were in Sandy Bay, remember?" She asked him sweetly.

"Yes, and I was late." He responded.

"Yeah." She said, her words staggered between shallow breaths.

 "It was snowing that night. The restaurant was packed. I left my name with the hostess so we could get a table and then was heading outside to have a smoke and wait for you." She said as she started to cough.

A few seconds of silence had gone by before Liam had looked down to see Anny slipping away again. Her head slumped on her shoulder.

"Anny, come on. What happened next?" He asked a little

louder to wake her. She rolled her head up straight again and continued.

"I got to the entrance and my phone went off. It took me forever to find the fucking thing in my huge purse, but I did. You had sent me a message," she said weakly.

What did it say?" Liam asked, already knowing the answer.

"It said, I'm at the restaurant." Anny answered. "Okay then what?" Liam asked trying to keep her talking. "I told you I was as well and asked where you were," Anny responded. "Then what happened?" Liam asked softly.

"You said looking at you. " Anny responded and then continued, "My heart stopped in my chest, and it took me a second to gather myself. I went back into the restaurant and scanned the faces, but didn't see yours. I came back into the entrance and looked through the glass door and saw you looking at me. I stopped dead in my tracks. You were standing in the parking lot in the glow of the street lights. The snow was falling softly around you. You were smiling, watching my every action and reaction to your words. It took my breath away and I knew I was in trouble."

"Why would you be in trouble?" he asked sweetly, never

having asked before, but wanting to keep her talking. "Because I knew in that moment that you were the only man I had ever truly been in love with in my life and it scared the shit out of me?" She said quietly. "Why were you scared?" he asked. "Because I knew that you owned my heart and that there was no turning back," she said and then closed her eyes.

Liam felt a twinge in his heart as he asked her, "Why have I never heard this part of the story?" He looked down at Anny to see her slumped over and motionless.

"Anny wake up! Wake up!" Liam shouted at her.

Liam looked ahead and saw an exit sign. He pulled off the highway and into a super centre, parking near the end of the lot beside an older model, late 80's, Chevy truck, "Anny, stay awake. I will be right back. I need to get some supplies. Promise me you will stay awake." He said. She lay limp, giving him no response.

As he pulled the keys out of the ignition, he caught a glance of his shirt and saw the blood. He looked closer and realized that he had completely forgot about his appearance. Scrambling, he looked over his shoulder to the back of the vehicle. Spotting his bag from the gym, he reached for it. He pulled out a dirty T shirt from the bag.

Looking in the rear view mirror he inspected his face. Licking his hand and rubbing off the blood he started to panic. *Concentrate Liam,* his inner voice was yelling at him, *this is no time to lose your cool.* He changed his shirt and gave Anny a shake but she was unresponsive. "Baby please wake up," he said, an air of desperation in his voice. She moved ever so slightly and groaned. He exited the vehicle and hurried towards the store, keeping his mind busy with the list of supplies he needed. *One outfit each including shoes, garbage bags, medical supplies, towels, water, cooler, ice, frozen peas, flashlight, pay as you go cell phone, sewing kit, map, gas cans, gas and alcohol.* He kept repeating the list over and over again to keep himself centred. Hurrying through the store, obtaining all the items but gas and alcohol, he reached the till. As he pulled out his debit card he caught himself. *I can't leave a trail,* he reminded himself. He checked the cash he had in his wallet and realized that he had only a couple hundred dollars left after the purchase. He grabbed the bags and receipt and hurried out the door. He headed to the vehicle and put the bags in. He made his way to the next two stops for gas and alcohol and returned to find Anny still not moving.

He opened the back door of the Suburban and retrieved a screw driver from his tool box. Moving quickly, he removed the plates from the vehicle and placed them inside, number side down. He hopped into the driver's seat and covered the VIN number with a takeout menu he had on his console. Leaning over Anny, he opened the glove box and retrieved his police issued 45 caliber Glock handgun, badge, extra ammo, and his vehicle registration. He shoved the items, his bloody T-shirt and Sonny's cell phone into gym bag and zipped it up. He scanned the parking lot to see if he could see anyone heading their way. Seeing no-one, he moved quickly. He walked to the passenger side of the truck he had parked next to, smashed out the small window, and reached in pulling the handle to unlock the door. He put the purchases in the back of the truck, placed the gym bag behind the seat, opened the drivers' side door, and then hurried to get the vehicle started. He popped the casing off the ignition, jammed the screw driver in hard, and turned it, starting the large V8 engine. He ran to retrieve Anny from the Suburban, locking the doors behind him. Buckling her into the passenger seat he shook her again. She opened her eyes and looked at him. "That's right, baby. Stay with me." he said, and kissed the top of her head. He jumped into the driver's seat and put the vehicle into drive.

"Don't worry, Anny. We're gonna be okay. I promise, we'll be okay." he said to her, as a sinking feeling washed over him. He pulled out of the parking lot and headed north, trying to convince himself of the truth in what he had just said.

Chapter Eight

*A*fter an hour of driving a deserted highway, Liam spotted a sign for a rest station. He pulled the truck in and checked for other occupants. Finding it empty, he let out a sigh. He got out of the truck, stretched his long legs, and breathed in a deep breath to clear his head. The last hour, his head had been spinning. He had been running through scenarios as he tried to figure out a solution for their predicament. He walked to the back of the truck, pulled out the map he had purchased from one of the bags, and looked it over, finding their approximate location. When he realized where he was on the map, he was hit suddenly with a plan.

He reached into the bag of items and pulled out the pay as you go cell phone. Ripping it from its wrapper, he hoped that the cigarette lighter port was still working in the truck. He reached into the truck and plugged it in. To his content, the light turned green. Liam breathed a sigh of relief. He opened a bottle of water from the cooler in the back of the truck, took a long swig, and scanned his surroundings. He noticed a bathroom facility, and decided to check to see if there was running water. Once inside, he found there to be and ensured its vacancy.

He returned to the truck and grabbed the clothing he had bought for Anny and a few other supplies. He brought them into the bathroom and then returned to the truck for her. While being unbuckled she started to stir. "Come on. We got to get you cleaned up." He said to her as he picked her up into his arms.

He carried her to the bathroom and sat her down on the floor. "Come on, sweetie. I need your help," he said trying to get her more alert. She sat up to the best of her abilities and looked at him.

"Where are we?" She asked.

"Nowhere anyone can find us right now, and that's all that

matters," he responded.

"Look at me. I need to clean your face. It's gonna hurt so just be prepared. Take these Advil and have a swig of rum."

She put the pills into her mouth and took a long swig from the bottle.

He kissed her forehead and then tried to gently wipe the dried blood from her face with a damp cloth.

"Owww" She winced.

"I have to stitch your face. Take another drink baby. This is gonna really hurt," he warned her. She took another drink and prepared herself. He sterilized the wound and then started to stitch her cheek that was mangled, attempting to stitch it ever so gently. "Mother Fucker!" She screamed out in pain.

"Come on. I thought you were a tough biker bitch," he teased her." We are almost done."

"Fucker," she teased him back and did her best to shoot him a dirty look, although her face was swollen and bruised.

Liam finished cleaning her face and then started on her arms. Realizing that her shoulder was dislocated, he prepared her for one last bout of pain.

"Okay baby, take one more drink. Make it a big one. This is really gonna fucking hurt but just for a second." He instructed her.

"Are you fucking kidding me?" She said, pain already in her voice. She chugged down half the bottle. Liam gave her a moment with hope that the alcohol would reach her system enough to numb the ensuing bolt of pain she was about to feel. He looked her in the eyes and asked, "Ready?"

She nodded her head, a look of fear in her eyes. He grabbed her hand and extended her arm, holding her collar bone hard against the wall. "Okay, look at me, one, two, three."

Anny screeched in pain as Liam in one fluid motion snapped her shoulder back into place. "Finish the bottle. That should be it for now, okay? You did good, baby," Liam reassured her.

Once she finished, he helped her to her feet. Though weak, she did her best to balance herself. He smiled at her, gave her a wink and then said in a sexy tone, "Now drop the robe, baby, and show me them curves."

Anny giggled softly and did as she was requested to do. Liam tried to hide his look of horror from her as he saw the damage from the altercation to her body. Black and yellow bruising was covering the majority of her upper torso. He could see the broken ribs and the swelling of the cuts to her back and legs. He worked fast trying to remove the dried blood that had been spilled from Sonny onto her chest and body ever so gently.

"A little different scenario than the last public bathroom rendezvous, eh babe," she said trying to lighten the situation.

"Ah yeah! I would say so, but hey at least I got ya naked this time!" He said and then laughed.

He reached into the shopping bag and pulled out the outfit he had bought for her. He helped her put on a pair of panties and then instructed her to lift her arms up as best she could. He slipped the summer dress over her head and ensured that it was straight. Kneeling on the floor in front of her, he helped her balance and put a pair of flip flops on her feet.

Anny looked down at the dress as she was being helped

with her shoes. "What the fuck is this?" She asked Liam

"What? What the fuck is what?" he asked in shock, but happy at the same time to see her much more lucid.

"This dress? What is this? It's baby blue and has daisies on it!" she reported.

"Really?" Liam retorted as he looked up at her. "This is your concern at this exact juncture in time, that you are not fashion forward. Well excuse me sweetheart but the skull and cross bones biker section was all empty at that particular Walmart. Go figure."

"Baby, you got me butterfly printed flip flops. I look like a fucking jackass," she laughed.

He stood up, shook his head, and pulled her into his arms, "Don't worry, baby. You look beautiful and none of the other prisoners on the cell block will be able to see your mug shot, okay. All the girls will love you and want you to be their girlfriend."

Anny burst out laughing, as she held her ribs and tied not to show her pain, and then responded, "Well that's all one can hope for. The strongest girl on D block to love and hold forever."

Liam kissed the top of her head and held her close. "I'm so glad you're back. I thought I was gonna lose you there for a bit."

Anny squeezed him with the little strength she had and responded, "Are you kidding me. You're not gonna get rid of me that easy!"

"He kissed her ever so gently on the cheek and said, "Okay, you're all done. Let's get you back to the truck. I gotta clean up too. I need you to keep watch and if anyone pulls in give the horn a quick tap."

He brought her back to the truck and handed her a bottle of water from the cooler and a frozen bag of pees to use on her face for the swelling. She sat keeping watch as he got himself in order in the bathroom. Leaning his backside against the sink, wiping his hands with the towel, he was deep in thought, going over the plan in his head. He packed up their bloody clothes and towels into a garbage bag and headed back outside. Finding a large metal trash can, he threw the bag into it. He grabbed one of the gas cans from the back of the truck and brought it to the can. Reaching inside the truck, he grabbed the gym bag from behind the seat. He threw the bloody T-shirt and vehicle registration into the can. He poured a small amount of gas over the bag and started it on fire. It took off in a flash. He then returned to the truck and emptied the remaining gas into the tank. He returned the bag back behind the seat, before he started the truck and pulled out of the parking lot.

"What are we going to do, Liam?" Anny asked suddenly, "Where are we going to go?"

"Don't worry Anny! I got a plan," he said as he tried to keep the worry from his tone, "We're gonna be alright. I won't let anything happen to you ever again baby! I promise."

Liam gave her a reassuring look and then turned on the radio and turned up the music. Both of them stared out the front windshield, quietly hoping their future would not be as dark as the evening sky ahead of them. Aware that their next moves would mean the difference between their demise and their survival.

Chapter Nine

*T*he high beams of the truck illuminated the trees that lined the long dirt driveway in an ominous way. It was two A.M. when they finally reached their destination. Navigating the many backroads, Liam had hoped that his memory would serve him well, and he would remember how to get to his father's old hunt camp. As they pulled up to the cabin, it was evident the place had been vacant for quite some time. The front porch sagged as though the home itself had decided upon retirement. The screen door looked as though it was holding on for dear life as it hung on an angle with only one hinge still intact. Liam pulled the truck up to one of the outbuildings, allowing the high beams to provide the necessary light he needed. He exited the vehicle, retrieved a flashlight and a screw driver from the back, and proceeded towards the shed. With a sharp thrust, he cracked the hinge that held the padlock on the door and removed it, allowing him entrance. He turned on the flashlight and stepped in. Anny watched as he disappeared into the building. *Where the hell are we...* was all she could think. Moments later, Liam returned and grabbed the last can of gas from the back of the truck.

"Let's hope I can get this generator to start, babe. Just give me a few minutes, okay?" he said to her. Anny nodded her head in response. After a few minutes of cursing and crashes she heard the motor turn over, sputtering at first and then holding its roar.

"Oh thank god!" Liam said with a tone of relief as he entered the truck. He reversed the vehicle and pulled up to the cabin shinning the lights upon it. "Okay just a few more minutes. Stay here. I'll be back." He instructed her before heading out of the vehicle and into the cabin. Anny sat in silence as she waited for Liam. Thoughts were racing through her head. *What have I done? What are we gonna do? Oh my god what about Cassy?* A twinge of pain radiated through her chest. The booze was wearing off. Exhaustion had overcome her as she repositioned herself. Moments later the cabin was lit up with the warm glow of lights. She looked up to see Liam in the doorway, waving for her to come in.

She slowly climbed out of the vehicle, using the door for leverage. Making her way up the rickety steps she stopped to catch her breath, holding her ribs to ease the sharp pains that now ran steady through her. Liam helped her into the cabin and sat her down at the table.

"Okay, baby just sit for a minute. Let me see what I can find to help," he said, trying to ease her pain. He looked through the cabinets, one by one, scanning their contents. Finally he saw what he had been searching for. He pulled out a bottle of Glenfiddich scotch and wiped off the dust. He cracked open the cap and handed it to her. "Take a swig babe. I'm gonna get the rest of the supplies from the truck and get some more Advil for you," he said and then disappeared out the door. Anny did as she was instructed to do. The scotch was smooth and it instantly numbed the back of her throat. She heard Liam close the door and place the cooler on the floor. As she turned to look at him tears welled up in her eyes.

"Liam I'm sorry! I am so sorry for all of this! I never meant for anything like this to happen! I just thought I could disappear. I didn't think Peter would do this. I'm so sorry!" Anny said as she began to cry.

Liam finished putting the items down and rushed to her.
He knelt in front of her and carefully held her. "This is not
your fault Anny! None of this is your fault! I'm gonna take
care of this. We are going to be okay, one way or another.
We just have to keep our shit together now. I need you to
pull yourself together. We both knew this wasn't going to
be easy, us being together, but we are gonna be okay. I
promise!" he said as he pulled himself away from her and
looked her in the eyes. "You trust me, don't you?"

"Yes, I trust you," she said gathering herself.

"Good, now let's get you to bed. You need to sleep," he
said. "Take some more Advil and a few more sips of scotch
while I get the bed ready." He handed her some Advil and
then headed to the bedroom. In the bedroom he searched
the closet and found a tote full of blankets. He flipped the
mattress and let the dust settle before doing his best to
make the bed with the musty blankets. Once finished, he
retrieved Anny and helped her to the bed. I gotta a few
things to do, then I'll be in," he said as he tucked her in and
kissed her forehead.

She grabbed his hand and looked up at him. Her face was
blackened and raw from the bruising. Please stay just until I
fall asleep." She asked quietly. He looked down at her and

recognized the fear that she was trying to hide. He crawled
into bed behind her, pulled her into him, and held her. As
he felt her start relax into him, he felt the tears burning in
his eyes. He tried to choke back the tears of anger as he
stroked her hair, and stared at her face as she slowly started
to drift off. *Never again baby! This will never happen again!* He
thought to himself as he tried to project through to her.

Once assured Anny was asleep, Liam pulled himself up
slowly from the bed as not to wake her. He grabbed the cell
phone and headed outside. He jumped into the truck and
started it, pulled it around the back of the cabin and behind
a wood shed; hiding it from general view. The last thing he
needed was a nosey neighbour calling in a possible
disturbance to the local police, only to have them pull in
and run the plates of the stolen truck. He headed inside and
finished unpacking the rest of the supplies he had
purchased. Looking through the kitchen, he did a quick
inventory of their goods. *Maybe a few days' worth of supplies,* he
told himself. The glow of the dawn caught his eye from the
window. He headed outside and turned off the generator,
to preserve what little gas was left for another round.

The glow of red and orange of the sunrise had started to
sweep through the tree line. The beauty of it drew him to it.
The sound of the morning calls of the forest seemed
amplified as the darkness was taken over by the new light

of day. He found a seat on a log overlooking the small pond that the property held, and watched as the day brought in a show of colours as through just for him. As he sat, the day's events flashed through his mind and he could no longer hold back his anger. Tears of rage ran down his face as he screamed at the sky as if to curse the world. He picked up anything he could find on the shoreline, and whipped it as hard as he could into the water. A fallen tree limb became a weapon upon the log that was once his peaceful stoop. He smashed it into a thousand pieces before exhaustion over took his arms. The once harmonized sounds of the nature around him, welcoming the day, had silenced as he slid to the ground resting his back on the broken log that he had taken his vengeance upon. He sat for the longest time in the silence, welcoming it, as he gathered himself.

His hands were throbbing from the impacts that had vibrated up the branch into his hands. He stared down at them, tried to will them to stop shaking, and for the burning of the splinters that had embedded themselves into his palms to subside. He let out a few deep breaths and pulled himself together, bringing himself up to a standing position. Walking away from the scene of his emotional decent, he started to go over his plan in his head to centre himself. *Secure Anny's'safety, Figure out an exit strategy for us. Find Cassy. Ensure her extraction.*

He headed back to the house and grabbed the half-drunk bottle of scotch from the kitchen table. Pouring some over his bloody palms he winced before swigging the remainder of the bottle down his throat. He picked up the cell phone, turned off the GPS, blocked the number and began to dial the number to the cell phone he had been dreading to call. The phone rang for the fourth ring before a half awake gruff voice answered, "Who the fuck is dead?"

"Sonny Omous," Liam answered, paused for a moment and then said, "Hi dad."

Jesus Christ, Liam! What the hell is going on?" His dad said sharply, "You're all over the news! Your mother is a wreck! Where are you? What the fuck happened?"

"Dad, I need your help. I'm at the duck hut. I need money and supplies. Call Stormy and Blue." Liam requested almost without emotion. "Liam, what? How?" His dad started to say.

"Dad, I've got no time to explain, your phone is probably already being monitored. I have never asked you for anything before. I need you now. Just trust me and let me know that I can trust. Okay?" Liam cut him off harshly.

He let out a deep sigh and then in response he said "Okay, son. Okay."

With that, Liam hung up the phone.

Chapter Ten

*T*he heat of the morning sun had started to penetrate the back of Liam's dark T-shirt as he hurried to search the truck for Sonny's cell phone. Ripping through the bag he had placed behind the seat, he felt it nestled in the bottom corner. He pulled it out and examined the phone. The dried blood had caked onto the screen. He carefully wiped it off and turned it on. Scanning through the call logs he found only one number on the phone. Taking a breath to calm his nerves, he centred himself before hitting the call button. As it rang, Liam felt tension travelling up his spine and anger twisting in his gut.

"Inspector Woods, I presume," Peter sneered quietly.

"You presume right," Liam responded harshly. "How's the hand these days, Peter?"

"Well I think of you every time it rains. Almost a romantic notion, don't ya think?" said Peter and then asked, "Where's Anny?"

"Anny's gone and she's never coming back. Where's Cassy Abraham?" Liam asked.

"Oh Cassy, yeah, she's just enjoying some quiet time right now. It's been an eventful couple weeks for the girl. Lots of late nights with the boys and such. You know how it is, a pretty girl like that always a good time." Peter half laughed into the phone and then screamed. "PROBABLY NOT AS MUCH FUN AS YOU'VE BEEN HAVING FUCKING MY OLD LADY THOUGH! YOU FUCKING DIRTY PIG! WHERE THE FUCK IS THAT WHORE?"

"I told you she's in the wind. You are never going to see her again, and you're right she is a lot of fun," Liam answered coldly, trying to rowel him up. "This beef is between you and me. Let's settle this one on one. All I want is Cassy. You let her go and we can finish this shit once and for all. No cops! No bullshit! Just you and me and only one of us leaves!"

"Like you got the fucking balls for that!" Peter voice snapped in Liam's ear.

"Fucking try me asshole! I got nothing left to lose. The women I love, my career, everything I had is gone because of you and your bullshit need to try and be some big fucking man. You hide behind your patch and bullshit brotherhood of thieves and thugs. I doubt you even have the ability to fight like a man with me. You're just a scared little boy who expects respect from all but gives none to any. I would love nothing better than to show you the full force of my disrespect for you. And when I'm finished with you, everyone will know what I've just said to be true," Liam stated plainly.

He heard Peter snicker into the phone, and then a pause of silence before he snarled, "You're on bitch. You got 48 hours to get to Toronto; dock 12 pier 3. You come alone. If I even think I see a cop, I'm gonna put a bullet in her pretty fucking face. Don't be late, hero!"

Liam turned off the phone and let out a long breath. His hands were shaking as he grabbed the bag from the truck and headed up toward the cabin. On the front porch he stood watching the sun filter through the trees, and taking a moment to calm his nerves. Once calm he entered the cabin. He loaded his police issued Glock and placed it on the bedside table. He laid with Anny, curling her into his arms. He held her tight into him, memorizing the feeling of her body next to his and the sweet smell of her. As he etched this into his brain, he felt his body relax and exhaustion flow over him. His eyes slowly shut as he fought the urge to drift off, warm and safe with Anny in his arms.

A slam of a vehicle door awoke Liam. He had slipped off into to sleep. He shot up from the bed and caught his bearings. He reached for his gun and made his way to the main room. Straddling himself in a hallway, he pointed the gun towards the front door. He could hear footsteps making their way up the porch. The doorknob turned slowly as he cocked his gun, preparing himself for the unknown. The door opened slowly and he could see stern, piercing blue eyes staring at him through it.

"Son put that fucking thing down before you make a mess out of something. Didn't your dad teach you anything? Damn it! What kind of fucking shit are you in now?" He heard Blue say in a condescending but half kidding tone.

Liam gave a sigh of relief and lowered his hand gun. Admittedly he was relieved to see Blue, who had always been a kind of uncle figure to him, even though he put him through the ringer every chance he could in a good old-fashioned military way. Blue, Stormy, and his father had established the hunt camp known as the "the duck hut" to the few who were ever invited there. It was a man's haven. The hunting was good, mostly bird (thus the name), but above and beyond it was a place for the men. Many bottles of scotch and steak dinners were had over stories of women and glory of fights won. Liam had been made privy at a young age and had always looked forward to the time away during summer and fall. He had looked up to Blue and Stormy and enjoyed their banter. They had always included him in a teasing manner. They had filled in for the spaces that he had felt distance between himself and his father in their relationship.

His father was as hard as they came. A military vet, he had seen his time in battle and did not take kindly to weakness in his son. It was part of their heritage, a linkage on the chain of previous wars fought, his father had found it necessary to serve, and had enlisted during the time of the Vietnam War. The Canadians were not involved. However, due to his persistence he found a way along with 30,000 other Canadians. He had joined the American forces through a loop hole in the government. Due to his skill set and perseverance was placed in the 129th ARG unit from California. This is where he had first met the men whose call names superseded them. Blue and Stormy had been on many missions with Fred who had been handled Haywire. They as well were among the few Canadians who had made the elite squad. The squad was originally established during the mid-1950's as an air resupply group. It had quickly changed during the Vietnam War. It became designated as a "Psychological Warfare" unit which supported unconventional warfare (guerrilla warfare), direct action (commando-type raids), and strategic reconnaissance (intelligence gathering). The three had seen many combats together and had kept ties. The hunt camp was a yearly ritual and a way of keeping in touch.

"Son what is going on? What sorta shit did you land in now?" Blue asked.

Liam let out a deep breath and placed his gun on the kitchen table. He sat himself down on a chair and tried to get his thoughts in order to explain the full context of the situation to Blue. He had always loved the man, and out of anyone he had never wanted to disappoint him. Memories of past times from childhood flashed through his mind; his first time firing a gun; the first time seeing a naked women in the magazines that were rampant amongst the camp; listening to the many wartime stories, some triumphant, some not, but all shed in darkness. He knew deep down that this place and these men were the reason that he had chosen the career he had. He knew that his guild was based on the stories he had heard of places where the breakdown of civil governance had led to unimaginable horrors. The last thing he wanted was to be thought of badly through the eyes of Blue. He let out a sigh and began to explain the last few years to him, hoping that he would understand.

"Okay! Okay! Let's get this into perspective," said Blue. "Right now it sounds as though you have an idea as to how to extract Cassy. We need to figure out a way to get you and Anny out of the country when you get back. Stormy is better at that sort of thing than me. He'll be here in a few hours with supplies. Let's take a look at your girl, and get you on the road."

"Thank you." Liam said, as he tried to hold back his emotions from Blue. He breathed in hard through his palm that was covering his mouth and lower face. He ran his fingers down his chin line and let out a deep sigh.

Blue stopped what he is doing and looked at him. He placed his hand on Liam's shoulder and looked at him sternly. He put his truck keys and a stack of money in front of him and said, "Son, it is what it is, until it isn't. This will all come out in the wash. You're a smart man. If you love her, and this is meant to be, it will be. That's what life's about, son. It's not about what you have or who other people think you are. It's about knowing who you are and accepting that. It's about relationships and allowing love into your life. I've seen many men die on the battlefield, and never in the end has any of them talked of their money or things. All they want is one more moment to see their children and the women they love. You go. Take care of your business! I got this! Know that I am proud of you for choosing your heart."

Liam looked up at Blue with a look of both determination and gratitude and nodded his head. "Thank you, sir!" he said and then got up and grabbed his bag and gun. He wrote down the phone number to Sonny's cell, and instructed Blue that he can be reached on it. With that, Liam exited the cabin, started the truck and drove away

Chapter Eleven

*L*iam cracked the window of the truck and allowed the fresh air to enter his lungs. The few hours of sleep he had at the cabin had not been enough. He needed to concentrate and keep his eyes on the road and his mind clear. He had made good time and had already made it halfway on his twenty hour drive from Savant Lake to Toronto. Keeping his eyes peeled for police and watching his speed so as to not draw attention to himself was a priority now. He saw a sign for a gas station and a Tim Horton's and decided to take advantage of the pit stop.

After filling up the truck and his stomach he reached for

his cell phone. He walked away from the truck and found a quiet spot away from the noise of the traffic from the highway. Taking a deep breath, he dialled the number to his Sargent. After three rings, he answered.

"Sargent Dalahan speaking," he heard the stern voice say into the phone.

"Hey Sarg, it's Liam." Liam responded quietly.

"Inspector Woods? Where the hell are you? Where is Anny Omous? You are in deep shit Inspector!" Sargent Dalahan yelled into the phone.

"I know sir, but it had to be done this way. Anny Omous is gone. I have made contact with Peter Wilson. I have arranged for an extraction for Cassy Abraham. This will happen today. I need to secure a plan for her safety and return home once this has happened. I will be trading myself for her. I need to know that a team will be ready when I alert you of my location. I have one shot at this. If he even suspects police involvement this will all go to hell and Mrs. Abraham and myself will most certainly pay the price," Liam responded.

"What the fuck are you talking about? Trading yourself, that's crazy! Why would you do that? You tell me the location of the meet now! I will have teams ready and waiting," Sargent Dalahan instructed him.

"I can guarantee you that they are, and have been, watching the area and the location. I must do it this way. Once I arrive, I will turn on the GPS on this phone. You have the number now. All I can tell you is it is in Toronto, near the lake. Have teams in that general vicinity ready. Once they have taken me, you can track my location through my phone. Once apprehended, you will have my testimony with regards to the Cassy Abraham case, and a forcible confinement of a police officer charge to nail him with. That fucker will never see the light of day again. As for Anny Omous and the Sonny Omous incident we will deal with that when this is done." Liam said in a calm and authoritative manner.

"Fine, but this better go down without a hitch, Inspector. If it doesn't you may not see the light of day again either. Do you understand me?" replied Sargent Dalahan.

"I know Sir! Trust me I know, but it's the only way," Liam replied. "I'll be seeing you soon, Sarg."

Liam hung up the phone. He walked back to the truck and paused for the longest time, staring out at the traffic. *This will work! This will work!* He told himself before taking a deep breath and entering the truck. *This will work! It has to!* He started the vehicle and pulled out of the parking lot, aware that his actions over the next few hours could possibly be his last.

Chapter Twelve

*T*he steady flow of traffic around Liam made the already present tension in his stomach grow. He had been going over his plan in his head consistently for the last two hours. The fast motion of the city had been a distraction and the reality of the upcoming event had begun to hit him hard. He did his best to swallow his emotions down into him, away from his mind.

Exiting off the freeway, he pulled over. He turned on his cell phone and turned on the GPS. He reached into his gym bag, grabbed Sonny's cell phone, took down Peter's telephone number, and shoved it into his pocket. Driving into the docks, he couldn't help but notice the area was vacant of workers. His adrenaline was pumping as he parked the truck at the agreed upon pier. He picked up his phone and dialled Peter's number. The phone picked up and Peter stayed silent on the other end.

"I'm here," Liam said calmly.

"I know," answered Peter.

Liam looked up and saw a black van reversing towards him from a few hundred feet away. The van stopped and the back doors were flung open, revealing a women bound with a black cloth bag on her head.

"Get out of your truck and slowly walk towards the van. Stop halfway," Peter instructed him. Doing as he was told, Liam exited the truck. He cradled the cell phone to his ear with his shoulder. His hands were busy holding his gun as he slowly walked towards the van pointing the gun forward and scanning his surroundings.

"Good, now stop right there." Peter told him. Liam stood waiting for Peter's next move. He heard a cry from the woman as she was shoved out of the van and onto the ground.

"Over here, Cassy. Follow my voice. Come to me," Liam shouted to her. She clumsily made her way up to her feet and walked towards him. Once close enough, Liam holstered his weapon and grabbed her. He felt her shaking as he untied her hands. He pulled the bag off her head and a sinking feeling washed over him. She started to laugh, and before he could gather himself she kneed him in the groin with all her might. While doubled over in pain and shock the women grabbed his gun. He looked up at her as she pointed his weapon at him. Realizing he had been tricked, he saw the women was not shaking out of fear, but rather with the twitching of junkie in need of a fix.

He heard fast approaching footsteps as he tried to gather himself, but it was too late. Pain shot through his body as he felt the multiple hits of fists and feet upon him. He curled himself into a fetal position on the ground, covering his face and head from the constant blows.

"That's enough boys, for now," he heard Peter's voice boom. "Search him! Take his cell phone."

All at once, the ambush had ended and Liam was roughly pulled to his feet, his arms pulled behind him with force. One man patted him down and finding no other weapons he picked up Liam's cell phone off the ground, and handed it to Peter.

"Thought you were pretty fucking smart eh? You probably thought you were gonna be in control of this! Didn't you? You fucking asshole. You really are a stupid fuck," Peter sneered at Liam.

He smashed Liam's cell phone on the ground and continued its destruction with the heal of his boot.

"Tie his hands and get him in the van, boys," he instructed the men, and then turned his back to Liam, motioning for the tweaker to come to him. She handed him the gun on her approach. Peter dug into his pocket, and pulled out a small bag of her fix and handed it to her. "Always a pleasure, Lily," he said. She made no reply as she scurried away quickly.

Six blocks away, Sargent Dalahan and his team sat restlessly in a surveillance van, carefully watching the GPS screen locating Liam's phone. Suddenly the red dot on the screen disappeared.

"Something's fucking wrong. ALL UNITS THIS IS A GO! ALL UNITS GO! GO! GO!" Dalahan yelled over the channel.

Peter could hear the sirens in the distance as he entered the van. "Get us the fuck out of here now!" He shouted at the driver. The tires squealed as they exited. Hitting the highway he yelled "Slow down and blend in!"

The driver did as he was told and headed west toward the 427 North highway exit.

Peter climbed into the back of the van with Liam and the other men. Liam sat silent, his hands bound behind his back, and a black bag covering his head and face.

"You sneaky mother fucker! I told you no cops. You just signed that bitch's death certificate," He screamed at Liam, pulling a hunting knife from his belt and plunging it into Liam's upper left thigh, "and your own!"

Liam felt the pain of the knife searing through his leg, then an impact to his head, and darkness.

"They're gone, Sarg!" said the constable upon approaching Sargent Dalahan.

"Get a chopper in the air now! Search every inch of this fucking place!"

Dalahan yelled at him. He looked down at the crushed cell phone and picked it up.

"We don't know what type of vehicle they're in. There's no point to a chopper Sir," the constable replied back.

"GOD DAM IT. FUCK!" Dalahan screamed. He heard his name being called from behind him and turned. "WHAT?"

"Sir we found this women behind one of the buildings shooting up. Should we take her in for questioning?" asked a uniformed officer towing the intoxicated women by the arm beside him.

"What do you think idiot? Of course bring her in! Listen up all of you," he said taking command. The team gathered around him awaiting their instructions. "This needs to happen fast. I want three of you working with unis searching this area. Two of you go with that fucking tweaker and question her. I want one of you to work on whatever you can get from this broken cell phone. The rest of you get teams prepared. I want warrants to search every fucking business and residence that is affiliated with this club. Get it done! NOW!"

He passed the cell phone to one of the men and walked away from the crowd. He drew in a deep breath, as he leaned his head up towards the sky, shaking his head and running his hands through his balding head. *Where the fuck are you Liam? Where the fuck are you?*

The light burned Liam's eyes as the bag was suddenly pulled off his head. He struggled trying to focus in, grateful to be able to draw air without effort. He looked around and took in his surroundings. The small cabin was filled with light from the large window in the open room. The scraping of a chair being dragged from behind him caught his attention.

Peter dragged the chair past Liam, in a slow manner, until he reached the other side of the table. He turned the chair backwards and plunked himself onto it facing Liam. He sat silent staring at him with a half snarl half smile upon his face, eyeing him up like prey. Liam sat silent, staring him straight in the eyes showing no fear.

"Where's Anny? I don't believe she is gone! In fact I believe she's still here. You know what I think? I think that she is going to look for you. I think she is going to come for you, and I think I am going to enjoy every minute of this," Peter said while studying Liam's face for a response.

"She's gone. I told you that. I don't even know where she is. So lets just get on with this," Liam replied as he slowly moved his wrists in the ropes, loosening their grip.

"BULLSHIT!!" Peter screamed, standing up and pounding his fists on the table. "You are going to fucking tell me where she is!"

He rushed at Liam, and as he did Liam with all his might pulled his hands apart and managed to free himself. He caught Peter and shoved him against the cupboards. His fist pounding into Peter with all his force to his face and upper body. Peter dropped to the ground and Liam continued with his attack, this time with his feet, kicking at Peter as he squirmed trying to avoid the impacts. Suddenly he felt himself being pulled away. The three other men had made it into the cabin after hearing the sounds. Liam forced one of them to the ground, punching him hard about the face. The two other men were on top of him, pulling him away, and hitting him over and over again. He struggled to get away from their grip on him, but was overwhelmed. They sat him back on the chair and bound his hands so tight he felt his circulation being cut off.

"Mother fucker!" Peter screeched at Liam as he pulled himself off the floor. He lunged at Liam, grabbing the knife that was imbedded in Liam's thigh. Liam let out a howl as Peter twisted the knife and embedded it deeper into him.

"You want to do this? Fine let's fucking do this!!" Peter screamed in Liam's face, wild eyed and crazed. He reached for a hammer that was on the counter. Liam prepared himself for the upcoming blow, as Peter wound the hammer up in the air to bring down upon him. Suddenly he stopped. The ringing of a cell phone that was not out of commission, had caught his attention.

"Where is that coming from?" Peter asked the men. They quietly all strained to listen, closely following the sound towards Liam.

"I thought I told you fuckers to search him. Get the fucking phone out of his pocket," he sneered at them. The young prospect did as he was told, retrieving the phone and handing it to Peter.

Peter answered the phone and stayed silent for a moment. He turned, looked at Liam and smiled before answering, "Hi love."

Liam looked up in horror at Peter. The only thought running through his head, *Oh god no! Anny no!*

Chapter Thirteen

I could hear the clanging of dishes and the smell of coffee brewing under the low hum of the generator as I tried to open my swollen eyes. The stinging was present but I could feel the swelling had come down enough for my lids to open. I attempted to roll over and felt the pain ripple through my ribs. Ever so slowly, I brought myself up to a sitting position and grabbed my mid-section to suppress the pain. I let out a long breath and then was suddenly aware of the muffled voices coming from the other room. As quietly as I could I stood up and made my way to the door. I opened the door slowly and silently. At the last moment the floor creaked beneath me, drawing attention to my direction. Fear tingled up my spine not knowing what I was about to encounter. *Oh god what if he found us!* I thought to myself as I turned to search for a hiding spot.

"Oh good you're alive. Don't be afraid, beautiful. We're here to help, "I heard a gruff voice call to me in a sweet manner. "It's okay. Come on out. Liam sent for us."

I turned around and faced the two older men who sat calmly at the kitchen table. It was apparent they had been there a while. The table was cluttered with cards strewn in piles across it, evidence that many hands had been played. Dishes, with half eaten sandwiches and chips, sat amongst them, along with a twelve gauge pump shot gun that lay pointing towards the front door.

My name is Blue," said the man with the piercing blue eyes and round face. "This here is Stormy," he said, pointing towards the small man with a slim face, covered in grey stubble. "He's a bit of prick but he grows on you." He continued on and then let out a deep belly laugh.

"Fuck you asshole," Stormy retorted. "Don't listen to this bastard, darling! I'm a gentleman. This is the slippery fuck you got to watch out for. He stood up, moved towards me, and extended his hand out to me in a welcoming gesture. I accepted his hand and shook it gently. He kept my hand in his and helped me towards the table. Sitting down I let out a groan trying to hold in the ensuing pain that would not seem to stop.

"Oh, we'll tape those for you. It'll help with some support. Here's some morphine pills. Take these they'll help in the in-term." Stormy said, as he clumsily tried to unscrew the cap on the pill bottle.

"Jesus, you're useless. Why the fuck do I keep you around?" Blue snapped at Stormy in a ribbing manner. "Go make the girl a coffee while I open that. What do you take in your rocket fuel girl?"

"Um, double double, thanks. Okay, this is weird. Who the hell are you guys, and where is Liam?" I asked as he handed me the pills and tried to move my dress up to examine my ribcage.

"You keep me around cause I saved your ass way too many fucking times!" Stormy said to Blue, "That, and you couldn't pick up a woman to save your fucking life; not even Thai hooker that was paid up front." He said laughing as he placed a coffee in front of me. He then looked at me and said, "Sorry for the language sweetheart."

"Yeah, watch your mouth you dirty old bastard. There's a

lady present," Blue said looking up at me and giving me a wink.

"OKAY! SERIOUSLY GENTELMAN WHERE IS LIAM AND WHAT IS HAPPENING HERE!" I questioned them in an authoritative tone, pushing Blue's hand off me. Both men sat down in their chairs and faced me. The smiles that once spread across their faces disappeared and a serious look took over both their demeanours.

"You're at our hunt camp; well ours and Fred's, Liam's dad. We're old friends of the family. Liam's gone. He went to go get your friend and straighten some things out with your ex. He'll be back in a day or so. Then we're going to get you guys out of the country," replied Blue in a serious tone.

"No! Oh god no! How could you let him leave! We need to call him right now and get him back here! He has no idea what he's walking into! One of you call him now, please!" I pleaded with them.

"You have nothing to worry about. Liam is a smart man. He knows what he's doing. Don't worry. He's a man of his word. He'll be back as soon as he can," Stormy said, trying to be reassuring.

"No! You don't understand. I know Liam is a man of his word. That's the problem! Peter is not. Liam stays true to his guild. He works off a set of honour and rules. Those rules do not apply to Peter. He's cunning and viscous. He will look for any weakness and use it against you to get the upper hand. He does not live by any rules other than that of his own survival and the needs the club. It'll be an ambush. He'll kill him! Just to spite me! He'll kill him!" I said trying to keep the tears in my eyes.

"Okay. Okay. Look we'll give him a quick call. You can talk to him and see you have nothing to worry about. Then we can go back to fixing you up and pleasantries." Blue picked up his phone and dialled the number. As it started to ring he handed the phone to me. I sat, every muscle in my body on edge, with the feeling of impending doom running the course of my veins. I heard the phone pick up.

"Liam, what are you doing? Please come back. Please don't do this!" I said, running through my words quickly.

I heard a breath on the other line and then a low snicker. I shot up from my seat, pain searing through my body.

"Hi love," I heard Peter say into the phone and then, " I missed you at the airport. I waited for you and you never showed up. Why would you do something like that? You left me standing there like some fucking asshole! You're my girl! You're mine! You know this! You belong to me! What would ever make you think you had the right to give yourself away to some FUCKING COP? You better get your ass home now, or I am going to cut out this fucker's heart and slice your girlfriend from one end to the next."

"This is all just a misunderstanding Peter! I'll come home! I'll explain everything! Please don't hurt them! This is all on me, baby. I made a mistake. I'm coming home and then we can just go back to where we were. Please let them go! Take it all out on me. Please, think of the club. You can't do this! You can't kill a cop like this! It'll bring the club down! Please, just let me come home, and we will figure this all out baby. I miss you." The words slid through my teeth like mud as I tried to convince him of my lies. I knew he was in a state of rage. If I could just convince him to stay calm, there was a chance I could secure a way out for Liam and Cassy.

I could see Blue and Stormy staring at me in disbelief at my words. I motioned my hand to them to hold on and shook my head with worry, waiting for a response from Peter. I could hear a scream in the background on the phone and a sound of a series of smashing sounds. All at once I heard Liam's voice yelling. Straining to hear through the noise of the altercation, I heard Liam cry out, "No! Anny, don't come here! Stay away!"

"You hear lover boy there? He doesn't want you to come. I do. I want you to witness what I am going to do to him. I want to show you how much you mean to me, so you know that you are mine, and that anyone who thinks that they can have you will suffer. Come home. Come home, and we'll work this out," Peter said in a distant tone.

"Okay! I'm coming. I need a few days Peter. I'm not well since seeing Sonny. Promise me you won't do anything until I get there. Please, promise me! I'll call you when I get close to Toronto. Promise me!" I bartered with him.

"Okay. Don't go home. The cops are watching. Just call me when you get close and I'll let you know where to go from there. Don't fuck me over Anny! If you fuck me over they both will be punished for you!" He warned me.

"I won't. I'll see you soon." With that I hung up the phone.

I handed the phone back to Blue slowly, and looked at them with panic. "They have him! I have to go! I need to go now!"

"What do you mean they have him?" Blue said looking at

me intently.

"I mean they fucking have him! I told you! You don't know who Peter is. I've seen him hit someone with a car for trying to talk to me. I have to go now, or Liam is dead." I stated almost without expression.

"No! We'll call the cops. This is too big. They can handle this. Liam is a big boy. He'll figure a way out of this. We'll call the cops! That's what we'll do," Stormy said with authority.

"No! We'll call Fred" Blue said to Stormy, "We'll call Fred and he'll figure this out. If we call the cops we will all be arrested!"

Realizing I wasn't get through to them, I took my only option. Swiftly I grabbed for the shot gun. It took every ounce of my strength to move the pump to cock the gun. The pain vibrated up my body with the motion. The sound caught their attention, stopping their rebuttal. They sat in silence in front of me.

"Now like I fucking said, I need to go now! You need to understand this. I will not leave Liam! When I was with Peter, on any given day, I would have taken a life if he had asked. Liam, for him I would give mine and I just might.

He is my heart, my soul, and my life. Without him I have none of these things and therefore am already dead. Now are you gonna fucking help me or not?" I said with stone cold conviction pointing the fire arm towards the door.

Stormy calmly looked at Blue and a smile spread across his face as he said, "Well Mister, I guess we're going on a road trip."

Chapter Fourteen

Cassy cringed as she watched the body of a large man roll down the stairs and hit the floor with a thud. She had been trying to block out the sounds of violence that seemed to never end above her. As the hatch door slammed and the sound of footsteps moved away from it, she let out a sigh of relief. She heard her new captive partner groan and the sound of him trying to stir.

"Hello? Are you okay?" She whispered towards the noise.

"Cassy? Is that you?" Liam responded in the darkness.

"Yes I'm Cassy. Who are you? Where are we?" She asked.

"It's Liam. Liam Woods." He responded.

"Liam? What the… why? Oh my god! You!" She said in broken sentences, piecing it together. "Anny went to you, didn't she? Where is she? Where are we? Are the police coming? Tell me we are getting out of here please!"

"I don't know where we are. I think north of the city. I know we are in the country. My plan didn't quite work out like I thought as I am sure you can tell. But don't worry. The R.C.M.P. are looking for us. I think Anny is on her way. I am sure she will call them as well. I hope! Either way we've got to start thinking of a plan just in case. I need your help. My leg is fucked! Can you move? I need you to help me take this knife out and bandage my leg. Then at least, I'll have a fighting chance next time they come down here for us." He asked her.

"Yeah, I can move, but I can't make out where you are. It's too dark," she responded.

"I have a lighter in my pocket. You need to get it out. I need you to take the knife out and use it to cut my hands free." He instructed her.

Cassy reached into his pocket and pulled out a lighter. She flicked it, and the room illuminated. He saw Cassys' face and the fear starting to leave her expression in the presence of a friend. She moved him and helped him lean up against the rock wall. Looking over his leg, she saw the knife embedded deep in his upper left thigh.

"We need something to bandage this up with after I pull it out." She said to him calmly. Cassy passed the lighter to Liam. He shifted himself to take it and maintained the light for them. She pulled off his belt and fastened it tight around his thigh above the wound. She pulled his shirt and ripped it length wise. He looked at Cassy. She looked at him, and he nodded his sign of readiness. She pulled hard on the knife moving it only part way out. "FUCK!" he screamed. "Okay! Just try a little harder, and get ready to put pressure on it."

She put her hand on the knife and prepared herself. With one sharp movement she yanked on the knife. He felt the blade scraping across the bone as she did. The knife released from his thigh and Liam let out a cry. Cassy scrambled to cover the wound and put as much pressure on it with what strength she could muster. The lighter, hot in Liam's hand, started to burn his thumb and he let the light go out to let it cool.

"You okay?" Cassy asks hesitantly. Liam breathed out a long breath and said, "Yeah, better. Thank you. I just need to sit here for a minute." They sat in the darkness together for what seemed like forever before they heard the sounds of loud voices shouting just outside the walls.

"You have to free my hands now!" Liam said to Cassy urgently. He lit the lighter again so she could see. She worked as fast as she could. Her one wounded hand throbbing as she tried to saw through the ropes. Finally she freed his hands. Liam let out a sigh of relief and rubbed his wrists. He handed the lighter to Cassy and took the shirt from her, wrapping it hard over the wound. He took the knife into his hand, gripping it tightly, as if not to lose it to the darkness that surrounded them.

"Put the lighter out and stay quiet," he whispered to her. She did as she was instructed. They sat together in the dark, listening intently to the conversation that had entered the building above them.

Peter had heard the sound of bikes long before he saw them coming up the long driveway, "Get this fucker downstairs now! I have a feeling this is Paul. The last thing we need is for him to know that we have him here." Peter instructed the other three men in his entourage. The men did as they were instructed and lift Liam to his feet. They teetered him sideways and allowed his own body weight and gravity to bring him down the stairs. Scrambling to clean up the scene, they moved the table over the port hatch and placed the chairs appropriately around it in an attempt to hide their actions of the last few hours.

"Get rid of the blood!" Peter yelled at them as he saw the bikes approaching fast with a cloud of dust in their wake. "I'll go great them. Act natural when we come in. Play some cards or fucking something. Crack a beer! Make it look normal." He snarled at them and then stomped out the front door. The screen slammed behind him as he made his way off the porch.

He watched the three men as they dismounted their bikes and approached him, taking off their helmets.

"Brother, to what do I owe the pleasure?" He smiled and asked as he greeted Paul with a hand shake, and a half hug followed by hard slaps to the back of manly affection.

"You tell me Peter! I've been hearing some fucked up shit. You got some civilian girl here? I hear you took her from the airport, and made some big fucking scene. Your bringing heat down on the club over your own personal bullshit. Is this right?" Paul asked sternly, gripping down on Peter's hand.

"You hear a lot rumours. I don't know what you're talking about!" Peter said trying to remain calm.

Paul released his hand and shoved him. "YOUR REALLY GONNA LIE TO ME RIGHT NOW? YOU FUCKING GOT SONNY KILLED! HOW THE FUCK DO YOU THINK I KNEW WHERE YOU WERE?" Paul screamed at him.

"CALM DOWN!" Peter yelled back at him. "YOU DON'T KNOW THE WHOLE STORY."

"DON'T YOU FUCKING YELL AT ME YOU PEICE OF SHIT! SHOW ME THE GIRL NOW!" Paul demanded.

The men moved into the cabin. Paul looked around and rolled his eyes at the feeble attempt at the cover up of the interrogation room. "Open the hatch now!" He instructed the prospects. The three men moved quickly to do as they were told, the fear of punishment fuelling their movements.

Paul peered down through the open hatch looking at the prisoners that the cellar held. He spun around facing Peter and yelled, "WHO THE FUCK IS THAT?"

Peter looked away not answering, and glared at his three accomplices ensuring their silence. Paul turned towards the young prospect and gritted his teeth. He sneered at him and asked him in a low voice, "Prospect, who the fuck is that?"

The young man, terrified for his life, blurted out, "Inspector Woods from the R.C.M.P."

"You little shit!" Peter screamed at the prospect. All at once, he felt the impact of Paul's might as his fist met Peter's face. Peter, taken aback, steadied himself against the kitchen counter in shock, holding his jaw as it throbbed.

"You're fucking done Peter! You crazy son of bitch! What the hell were you thinking taking a cop? You're finished," he said to Peter. He turned to his own escorts and continued to say, "Take his patch! Take all of theirs! Get these people out of here. Take them out back and get rid of them and any evidence they were here."

As the men approached Peter he reached into his jacket. Pulling out his forty five calibre hand gun he pointed it at Paul's head, "I don't fucking think so. No one calls me crazy."

A loud bang and a spray of red filled the room. Peter

turned and let a round enter into two of the men that had arrived with Paul. He spared the last one. He turned his attention to the young prospect that had given him up. The man shook with shock and fear. "Wrong move, asshole!" he screamed and squeezed out a round that entered the prospect's chest.

The room remained silent other than the ringing in their ears. Once it had subsided, Peter started to pace the room. "Let this be a lesson to all of you! Don't ever fuck with me!" He snarled still pacing, amped with adrenaline. He moved over to Paul and pulled his jacket off him. Wiping the blood off the front that showed his presidents' patch, he looked at the men in the room. He took off his leather and put on Paul's, "There will be no vote. Anyone who disputes this decision will die like they did. I'm president now. Any of you fuckers got a problem with that?"

The room stayed silent as Peter calmly stepped over the body of Paul, lit a smoke, and headed out the door, gun in hand.

Chapter Fifteen

The highway seemed to have more bumps than I could handle, and the old beast of a truck seemed to hit every single one of them. At least the morphine had kicked in and the taping of my ribs seemed to help with the impacts. I sat between Stormy and Blue staring out the windshield going over the events of the past last few days. All I could focus on was Liam and Cassy. *How could I have let this happen? I was responsible for all of this! I will get them out of this! Come hell or high water, they would survive this!* I told myself.

"What's the plan Anny?" I was suddenly shot from my thoughts as Stormy posed the question to me.

"Can I have your phone? I need to make a call," I asked. Stormy took one hand off the steering wheel and reached into his pocket to retrieve his phone. He looked at me with concern as he handed it to me. I dialled the number to my cousin Chances' cell phone, hoping he would answer. To my relief, he did.

"Hello," he said into the phone.

"Chance? It's me Anny," I answered.

"Anny! Holy fuck! Are you okay? You're all over the news, girl! What the fuck happened?" Chance questioned me.

"Chance, I need your help! Your dad's dead. I killed him. Peter sent him after me. I had no choice. He has my friends. One of them is a cop. He's lost his fucking mind! I need you to get a hold of Uncle Theo. I need to talk to him. Will you help me?" I responded quietly.

"Of course! Where are you?" Chance said without hesitation, and then asked, "Is it true you stabbed Sonny in the dick?"

"I'll be there soon! Yes I did. I had no choice," I answered.

"Okay, be careful Anny! Oh, and thanks. That fucker deserved what he got!" With that, he hung up the phone.

I handed the phone back to Stormy with a nod of thanks. He took it from me and asked, "So where to?"

"Barrie. We are going to Barrie. I'm gonna try and sleep for the next couple of hours, fellas. Okay?" I responded with a yawn.

I laid my head back onto the seat, scrunching myself down and finding a comfortable spot between the two men. I could feel myself drifting off. I concentrated, trying to remember every detail of Liam's face as I started to fall asleep.

It was twilight when I was nudged to wake. We had arrived in Barrie. I directed Stormy on where to go. Pulling into my cousin's driveway, I felt relief of being free of the cramped accommodations of the truck. I saw the outside light turn on as I exited the vehicle.

"Thanks fellas! I'll call you tomorrow morning okay? You're going to get a hold of Liam's dad and get him on board for this?" I asked.

"You bet, darling!" Blue answered back and winked.

"You got my number right?"

"Yep I got it. Oh, I'm gonna borrow this if you don't mind," I said as I snatched up the shot gun.

"She's all yours. Talk to you in the morning." Stormy said as he waved to Chance who had made his way outside.

I waved goodbye as they drove away, and then made my way up to Chance. Stepping into the light I could see the look of horror cross his face at my appearance. I winced as he grabbed me in for a hug.

"Oh, shit sorry. Holly shit Anny! You look like raw meat," he blurted out.

"Thanks! That's a great way to make a girl feel pretty, ya jerk," I giggled at him.

He started to laugh and then caught himself enough to look at me and asked, "What the fuck are you wearing?"

"Don't ask! I'm gonna have to borrow something to wear from Isabelle. If that's okay?" I responded chuckling.

"She's got a shift tonight, but you can borrow whatever you

want," He said as we entered the house.

I sat down at the kitchen table, placing the gun down on it, as he offered me a beer. "So what's the plan Anny?" he asked.

"Did you get a hold of Uncle Theo?" I asked him back.

"Yep, I did. You were right! There's some fucked up shit going on right now. No one knows where Paul is. Peter is M.I.A. as well, but there's rumours he's the reason the cops are all hot and horny right now to search everyone's houses. They're ripping through everything, the clubhouse, and every person or business that's connected to the club. They already laid charges on nine members so far. Everyone is flipping out," he answered.

"You didn't tell him I'm here, right?" I asked, suddenly aware of my close proximity to the city.

"Fuck no! What, do you think I'm an idiot? No, I just said I heard shit was going down, and I wanted to know if anyone had any idea about what happened to my dad. He wants to have a beer. I thought maybe you could talk to him then. He'll be alone so between the two of us, nothing's gonna happen," he set me straight.

"Awesome! You rock!" I said stretching my back out and yawning. "Listen I'm gonna grab a shower and head to bed. We got a lot of shit to figure out tomorrow."

"Cool! The spare room is all set up for ya. Glad to see ya cous'. Even if you do look like hell." He said and laughed. I finished the last swig of my beer and shot him a dirty look back in jest. With that I said my good nights, grabbed the gun, and headed off to clean myself up and get some rest.

The hot morning sun woke me from my sleep. I rolled up carefully and got out of bed. My sleep had been broken by the thoughts of the day's upcoming events rolling through my head at a furious pace. I headed downstairs and was grateful to find the coffee already brewed. I made my way outside to the back deck to join Chance who had already found his comfortable morning spot. Stealing one of his smokes, I lit it as I sank down into a comfy deck chair. We sat for the longest time in quiet looking out over the gardens in his backyard. After finishing my coffee, I asked Chance to borrow his phone. I needed to call Peter. He handed me his phone as I tried to calm myself enough to make the call. Dialling the number, my hands were shaking. After two rings the phone picked up. The silence on the other end only caused my anxiety to increase as I tried to contain my composure to spew out the lies I needed to say.

"Hi baby, it's me. I'll be in Toronto in two days. It took me some time to find a way there. My face is all over the news. Where am I going when I get there?" I said sweetly, trying to sound convincing.

"Don't go to Toronto. Head to the Muskoka's. Call me when you reach Huntsville and I'll give you directions. Don't fuck me over Anny! I'm giving you a chance here to make this right!" he answered back in a low tone.

"I won't, baby. It's just gonna be you and me, like it should have been. This is all just a big mistake. You'll see. I'll fix all of this. I love you." I said trying not to choke on my words. I needed to keep him calm and focused.

"I love you too," he said and then hung up the phone.

I could see the look of concern on Chance's face as I handed him back the phone. "You know this is a trap, Anny. You do know this, right?" he asked me in a serious tone.

"I know, but it's gonna be a trap for him," I said and gave him a serious look.

"What are you going to do Anny?" he asked grimly.

I stole another smoke and lit it, staring off at the gardens for the longest time before responding, "I'm gonna kill him. I'm gonna fucking kill them all."

REDEMPTION

By Anny Omous

INTRO

*H*is lips caressed mine eagerly: warm, soft, and with urgency, on my neck as he made his way with his mouth moving downward asking me to give into him. I opened my eyes to see his beautiful brown eyes gazing into mine, as if to question my loyalty. My eyes answer, yes. I feel his strong arms and hands lift me from my position and spin me to an equal level. I gaze into his eyes as I slowly move over him. He; in pleasure, moans escaping his lips. I feel his hands grasp my waist and travel down my hips. His breath changes and I feel him giving himself over to me. I feel pleasure in his wanting. I want only to fill his need; to feel him release; to feel him give himself to me. I continue to wake his urgency. I feel him awaken under me and release. Vibrations run through my body as we solidify our connection. He is mine, and I am his. For a moment we are one.

"Anny Wake up! We're here." I heard Blue say as I was nudged to consciousness. "It's time darling."

I sat up and blinked my eyes; trying to focus in. I looked ahead at the bush line, humbled by the dusk, as an impending feeling of doom swept over my body. The adrenaline coursing my veins prompted my engagement to the situation. Running over the next course of action, it fills my mind to its every corner.

"It's time." I hear Haywire say from behind me ripping me from my mind.

"I fucking heard him the first time." I retort trying to keep my calm.

"Let's go boys! Find your positions and text me when we are ready. We have no room for error here. Time to make it all worthwhile." I say calm as a nun.

"We got your back Anny. You got this. Make it count darling." Stormy whispers in my ear and pulls me in for a hug and a sweet kiss of encouragement to the cheek.

Trying to hide the shaking of my body I exited the vehicle. A quick nod of encouragement was received by all. I turned toward the bush line and walked towards it; I weaponless, and soul as naked as can be, knowing that my next actions would determine who lived and who died.

The Three Year Affair Series

By: Anny Omous

The Three Year Affair

The Guild

Redemption

Coming soon:

The Darkness

The River Boy

www.ingramcontent.com/pod-product-compliance
Lightning Source LLC
Chambersburg PA
CBHW052206170626
46812CB00004B/1679